Dre

by
Tom Wallace

Other books by Tom Wallace:

Conatus

Twenty-One Levels of Self-Deception

Three Miles of Rice Pudding

Utopia Governance and the Commons

A Little Book about Climate Change

Wild Body Wild Nature

Tales from a Distant Shore

Table of Contents

Yggdrasil

Yggdrasil is no ordinary tree, but the key to understanding heaven, hell and the lives we lead between the two....

A tree on three levels, they call me! Heaven, Earth and Hell. My roots in Hell, my branches in Heaven and the creatures of the Earth dancing around my trunk.

And who came up with that explanation? Yes, you've guessed it – the humans! They always want to split things up into yes and no, either, or, this and that, black and white, right and wrong. It gets them into a lot of trouble. At least, with me, they came up with three things. But they're still stuck with the same problem.

The world is not divided into two or three – the world is one.

Yes, I'm one tree! Don't try to chop me into parts, the way you do with everything else in life, you humans!

Let's start with Hell.

It's a puzzle to me why you humans always think the universe is going to punish you! Most of your problems are your own fault, but you always want to blame someone else for them.

And when you can't find a suitable victim on Earth then you blame God or the Devil or Fate or the Universe. What's wrong with accepting that there is Chance, Randomness and Chaos in the Universe, just as much as there is Grace and Beauty? Yes, bad things happen, but no, you do not need to blame, let alone punish anyone or anything for this. Remember it is from Chaos that all Order, Life, Beauty and Truth emerges. That is the way of the Universe. That is where I have my roots.

Then let's talk about Heaven.

Somehow you always think it's a long way off! Somehow you think you must earn your place. It is a labour for you. It is a burden in this life and then Heaven arrives only when you are dead! You leave it in the hands of the gods, or One God, or the Universe to make Heaven for you. You do not see that Heaven is within you. That it is already here for you as a gift. That you have the responsibility to receive this gift as a gift of Grace and to pass on that Grace to others. To make Heaven for others. Heaven is my branches, and my branches reach down to the Earth!

What then of Earth itself?

You think of it as a separate realm, shut off from both Heaven and Hell. But no! Think of it rather as somewhere where Heaven and Hell meet up and are mixed. So there's Chaos and then there's Cosmos. Randomness, pain, sorrow – the ripples of Chaos – mixed with Grace and Beauty – the adornment of Cosmos. Take up those difficult things that Chaos brings and then turn them around! If fearful, look after others who are in fear. If grieving, look after others who grieve. If melancholic, look after others who share in your melancholy. In all this, be kind.

I am one tree – Yggdrasil – and the world is one. Honour your gifts, you humans. Be Grace for the world.

DREAMTREE

The Tree Speaks

The tree of life feels that it's been misunderstood....

I am the tree of life! Come, eat of my fruit!
It's been a long time since you approached me, and I'm going to tell you why.
The myths you've been told get it wrong. For many thousands of years humans lived in peace and prosperity. I was there in your midst. The Goddess was worshipped, men and women were in harmony. Few, if any, lived in poverty or fear. Women were blessed with the wisdom to guide, council and heal. Women made sure everyone ate of my fruit.
But then something went wrong with one half of humanity.
Gradually men usurped their place in human culture. At first they just used their superior physical strength to upset the balance. But then they began making weapons to enforce their power. And the world was turned upside down!
They invented myths to try to convince all of humanity of their right to dominance and violence. Their greatest myth was the myth of the one who sought to replace the Goddess, the

one who sought to crush the heads of her sacred beings. The one who sought to debase and humiliate the feminine.

The new myths forbade humans to eat of my fruit – and the fruit of my sister tree, the tree of knowledge of good and evil. But women could never obey this nonsense as it is against the will of the Goddess. So the story was told that angels with flaming swords guard me from you. But there are no angels of death or angels with swords. This is the lie that you have been sold. And they say that one day I will be set in the midst of a great walled city and only a chosen few will be able to get to me. But once again, this is a lie. I am here for everyone.

10,000 years have passed since all this began. 10,000 years wasted. 10,000 years when men have raped, murdered and humiliated women. 10,000 years of ever more terrible war and the weapons of war. 10,000 years when the Goddess has been forgotten. 10,000 years when her creation has been pillaged, polluted and destroyed.

But I am still here. Waiting.

There was one however who understood. At least one.

New wine – he promised – the kingdom of Heaven within you! That new golden city (always a symbol of the feminine) resting not in some far distant place but right in your heart. And I would be there, constantly bearing fruit. You see, that was the way it once was and the way it really is right now! Can you hear that man's words and not wonder at the contrast with that angry faith the ministers of religion seem to promote?

The man cursed a fig tree once. It was not bearing figs, but it was not the season for figs.

What do the ministers say of this? They blame
you, that's what they say! But look at it another
way.   He was saying there should always be
fruit! My fruit!
So there it is. New wine. The fruit of life. The
kingdom of Heaven. All of that is open to you
right now!
Those ministers of religion – if they believe in
that man – have to square the circle. How can
they square the angry God who would crush the
head of the serpent with the gentle man who
would bring you back to the tree of life? But if
they succeeded, what a victory that would be!
I am the tree of life! Come, eat of my fruit!

The Knowledge

A young woman awakes confused after eating a mysterious fruit.

I open my eyes and at first I see only flashing lights. It is sunshine, I realise, as my mind gradually adjusts. Sunshine through leaves. I'm looking up into the trees. I raise my head a little and look down at my body. Breasts, belly, thighs, toes – I feel the life force flowing into my fingers and toes. Wasn't it always thus? I think. Don't I always sleep naked beneath the trees? Doesn't everyone, at least when the weather is fine? But something is different this morning. I'm more aware of my body, for one thing. I roll over onto my stomach, kick my legs a little, take some deep breaths, wiggle my hips.

And there is something I must do! Something I have somehow forgotten.

Memories come back slowly. Last night I wandered off alone. I felt the last rays of the sun on my skin and lay down in this shady glade for the night. A sacred creature had appeared, slithered past me and then up the trunk of a tree. A fruit had fallen at my feet and I had picked it up and eaten it without a second thought.

Was it that fruit that had made me forgetful? What is it that I should be doing?

Then recollections begin to come to me.

My childhood, under tuition of the priestess. We wore long yellow shifts as children, except when we were playing or swimming or sleeping under the trees on warmer nights. As girls we had sacred duties, the priestess had told us. To learn all the plants and herbs, flowers and trees and their uses for healing and nourishment. To care for our bodies as sacred and the bearers of new life. To teach the boys and men, because the male could be unruly and too literal and likely to go astray unless carefully tended.

It had been boring, she had to admit! As a child it hadn't meant that much, but gradually the teaching had sunk in.

There are three stages of the Goddess, she remembered now – the Maiden, the Mother and the Crone. But wasn't she still just a child? No, surely not! Too old for that by now.

Women kept the light in their hearts, in their minds, like a sacred city, built on a hill. Women carry humanity forward. Keep us at one with Nature. Broker peace with the Universe of Chaos. Act as ambassadors for the gifts of Grace that the Cosmos bestows.

There is a white robe for the maiden as she takes up her duties and helps teach the children. The knowledge she needed seemed to be inside her now somehow, in a way she could not explain.

She felt tired again, all of a sudden. It was still early. Perhaps she would just have a nap now, then get up and find her parents and sisters.

...

The old crone, in her dark blue robe, was

watching Eve from a nearby thicket of trees. She had seen her wake up with that puzzled look on her face, lie there thinking for a while, then, looking satisfied, rolling over for a nap.

She'd been a troubling pupil, that one. Wilful. Impetuous. Almost like a boy. But such a strong spirit! Now that she had eaten from the Tree of Knowledge, she would be a worthy maiden, a strong leader for the young.

The crone tipped back her dark blue hood and looked at the sky, thanking the Goddess for another day and for another woman to guide the world. Then she unfolded the white robe, ready to give it to Eve when she awoke.

Alone in the Wood

Sitting alone in the wood, you might just catch a conversation amongst the leaves and branches...

The night is warm. There is a full moon and only a light breeze.
It is nights like these that I love the most.
It is nights like these that the trees come alive.
I take my jacket off quickly and sit down on it in my favourite little grove of trees. No-one can find me here. No-one knows I come here. It is a secret between me and the trees.
Of course, when I say the trees come alive, I don't mean that they get up and walk around! No, but trees are different at night. That's what I'm meaning. Their branches nod slightly, and it's more than just because of the wind. Their leaves rustle a little. The trees seem to bend in closer to each other and have a conversation.
And if you are very lucky and you listen long enough, you can join in.
Well, you might not believe me when I tell you that trees talk – or let's say, converse. If you do believe me then maybe your next question would be: So, what do they talk about?

The answer is a bit complicated.

First of all, you need to know that trees lead a kind of double life. What goes on below ground is very different from what goes on above. Underground there's a whole communication network of roots and fungus that keeps forests chattering constantly. Trees don't do so well alone. They need all that support from the underground network – the Mycelium network, as it's called – in order to grow well. But this is a foreign language to us humans, too different from us to make any sense.

It's what goes on in the leaves and branches that is the most interesting side of things.

Because trees, being long-lived creatures, are very slow in their thoughts. The chatter below ground is rather like breathing or digestion or blood flow for humans. It's automatic and quick. But above ground the tree sits often through long winters or it might sit in a tropical forest where one day follows another with very little variation.

So the trees get to pondering the big questions. Why are we here at all? What happened when the Earth was just starting out as a new planet? What will happen in the future? Can the course of history (and they really mean geological history) be changed?

The trees, you see, are philosophers!

And they've plenty of time to think these thoughts – time on their branches, you could say!

But now you'll be asking me, what answers do the trees give to these questions?

Again this takes a bit of explaining.

For one thing, trees don't have words like us. They don't even think in images. Now imagine what it would be like for us to try to think without either words or pictures. It's all but impossible for us to do this. But still, our minds can function at a deeper level, below the words and pictures we usually think of as thought. That's why a 'solution' to a question can suddenly pop into our heads as if from nowhere. A deeper type of thought has been going on all the time, somewhere below the surface of our minds. It's this kind of deeper thought that we share with the trees, and indeed with all types of life.

The second thing to say is that trees don't look for answers in the way humans do. For humans there is always a question or a problem and the expectation that there will be an answer. But as I've said, trees don't so much think as contemplate. To contemplate something is not the same as trying to find an answer to it. To contemplate is to turn something over in our thoughts.

Now here's the really difficult bit. The things we think about, the things we contemplate, are not really separate from us. When we turn our attention to something we start to become that thing! And the more we contemplate something the closer we resemble it and the closer it resembles us.

So you could say the trees are the meaning that is in the world. They are the young Earth newly sprung to life and they are the future of our planet. Trees are the changes the planet will see as it grows old.

We humans are short-lived, furtive and restless creatures compared with trees. But if we slow down and take time to listen, we can share in those great things that the trees contemplate. And in some small way, at some deep level in our minds, we too can become those great

thoughts about life and meaning.
This is what it means to talk to trees.

DREAMTREE

Last Tree Standing

A solitary tree shares her thoughts on humans and forests....

I was a seed and then a sapling once in a vast forest. I felt the care and help of all the older trees around me – you see, we don't compete, as you might think. Instead we co-operate, so that every tree can be the best it could ever be.

A forest is an economy built on trust. A forest will never let you down. Unless there is no choice.

So together we had survived floods and droughts, fires and ice, torrents of rain and deep snow. We endured. We survived. Together we thrived.

But well, you know of course where that wave of destruction came from – the destruction that we could not survive.

Slowly my fellow trees were picked off one by one. Now I stand alone in a barren wilderness where almost nothing grows. On the horizon I see smoke and I hear what sounds like roaring thunder every day.

Why was I left? Why am I the last tree standing? It seems like it was just an accident, just bad luck or fate.

Perhaps you feel sorry for me now, given what I've told you? But don't feel sorry. Save your pity for yourselves, for we trees were built to endure.

You might think, if you dug into the soil around my trunk, that there's not much there. Just a bunch of microbes, but no larger life. And you might think, looking up at my almost naked branches, that there is little hope of flower or fruit or even leaves.

But if you think these thoughts then you don't know the power of nature. You do not realise that life can spring forth in abundance when nature knows that the time is right.

So I stand tall in my solitude and I endure. Because I know the age of the forests will come again. It may be in a century. It may take a thousand years. I may not survive to see it. But I know it will happen.

But for you it is different. Your days really are numbered. Each of you stands as if you are solitary trees! Independent, you say of yourselves. Autonomous. Free. And of this you are fiercely proud! You don't see the vast forests of land, sea and air that even now support you. So nature might come to think of you as a failed experiment. And get rid of you – or let you get rid of yourselves.

Are you going to take advice from a tree?

And I don't mean my words to be harsh. Let me tell you that we once had hope for you. We once thought of you as a great leap forward in nature.

And it could still be so. There is still time.

You could stop living like a cancer and start living like a forest.

Mycelium

Beneath the ground there's a lot going on. The underground network is trying to tell us something....

It took you long enough even to notice that I'm here!
Right under your noses.   Right under the ground.
And not just some bits of ground.   Every bit of ground!
Then once you'd discovered me – christening me with the name Mycelium Network – you got to explaining me as some kind of interaction of roots and fungus.   A chemical exchange.   An automatic process.
Phaaah!
Everything's got to be an automatic process for you, hasn't it?   Even your own minds, hearts, souls!   You seem to take comfort from the idea that you're an accident and the only intelligent life in the universe.   Why are you so attached to this idea of being alone?
Well, let me tell you that you're not alone. You're very far from being alone!
Because I'm not just underground, I'm

everywhere.

My network, as you call it, spreads down into rock and magma, into the core of the Earth itself. And I spread up into air, through leaves and branches, then out. Out beyond the atmosphere.

Space is not empty, as you so naively assume. Space teems with life and intelligence. So here on Earth I feel the pulse of life throughout the solar system, then out across the 'interstellar void' to Alpha Centauri and beyond.

The whole galaxy is thinking and breathing. Feeling. Hoping.

Well, if you accept this, you'll be asking, what is it that is hoped for? What does the Mycelium want?

I can only say that we hope for a lot of things, but as regards you, we hope you'll come back.

Okay, so now you're asking, come back from where?

That question takes a bit of unpacking.

First, look around at all the creatures you know on Earth. For so long you have thought of them as predator and prey, all engaged in violent competition in order to be 'survivors'. But whilst there's competition, there's also co-operation. Even the lion stalking the antelope is in 'co-operation' of a sort. Gradually, you've come to recognise this. Gradually you've come to understand that there are different types of intelligence, each suited to a particular way of living. You've seen the intelligence of animals, birds, fish and insects. Finally you've learnt the wisdom of trees and plants. Eventually you might graciously extend the reach of intelligence to include me!

So you could say the hope is co-operation. You were once in tune with nature. We just hope you'll learn to be that way again, but now with even greater wisdom. Learn to live in harmony with each other. Learn to live in harmony with the planet.

It's not so difficult. Because of course, we are part of you too. You are the Mycelium Network. So let's get to work.

Wood from the Trees

If a forest could speak, what might it tell us....

It's always black and white with you. Yes and no. True or false. Fact or fiction. Everything is a competition. But at last you have realised that co-operation is an alternative to all that competing.

But I must tell you that even that wider distinction of competition or co-operation is just a myth. For a forest, these distinctions don't mean very much. What you think of as truth today will be myth tomorrow. And tomorrow's truth will likewise change into myth and then be forgotten.

Some of you sit amongst my trees. And if you are wise you listen closely and hear the big thoughts about the past and the future and the purpose of it all. There's some wisdom there.

The wiser amongst you choose to live among trees, even in tree houses. And here you learn that there are other ways of knowing, other ways of being in the world. You learn that the connections in a forest that you thought took place underground are really extended outwards – even outwards into space.

You learn a greater wisdom from this. You might even learn to live like a forest. But you've not yet learnt to think like a forest.

Yes, I have to tell you that you just get the wrong impression of trees! For instance, in winter, when branches are bare, you think we are sad. Then you think we come alive in spring and summer and you think we're happy! If you cut down trees you might feel guilty. If you plant seeds or saplings you might think you're doing a good turn.

It's the same amongst yourselves. One is happy, another sad. One is thought to be doing good, another is bad. Black, white. Yes, no. True, false. Fact, fiction.

You need to live amongst trees to know a different way. I will not say a 'better' way, or a 'true' way, or a 'correct' way because, as you've probably guessed by now, those distinctions don't mean very much. Here's how I might describe it for a human. Every one of you lives by their own myth, or at least with the myth that they currently think of as the truth. So first of all, realise that this is who you are. And secondly, the most important thing – let others own their own myth. This, you'll appreciate, is a very tricky step. Because it doesn't mean not having an opinion. It really means just saying what you think and being completely happy, or completely indifferent, as to whether other people agree with you or not.

And the final thing to tell you about other people's myths is that all this doesn't mean you don't listen to what other people are saying. In fact, you listen very, very carefully to other people's myths. You contemplate the myths of others – not just sometimes but almost constantly.

If you can do all that then you'll start to think like a forest. You'll see the wood from the trees.

Sunflowers

*Resting amongst sunflowers on a summer's day
leads to thoughts about desire and pleasure.*

There's something deliciously exuberant and
indulgent about sunflowers! They are flowers to
the max! The uber-flower! No wonder insects
get dizzy with ecstasy when they visit flowers!
There's a field of sunflowers near my house.
Some of them have spilled over into a little
hollow in the ground next to the field, beneath a
tree. In summer it's a wonderful place to lie
down and read or sunbathe or just look at the
sky. A bank of moss, short grass and tiny
daisies sits amongst the rogue sunflowers that
have escaped from the field. I lie down on it
with my feet pointing upwards towards the sky.
It's a steep bank so it's almost like hanging
upside down. Sometimes it's good to see the
world the wrong way up.
Because there's something wrong with the
world, I'm thinking on this particular day. It has
too much knowledge perhaps, or too many
'facts' or people who think they know the facts.
Everyone has their own myth, and that's okay.
But why can't we just leave other people with

33

their myths and stick to ours without having to disagree? That seems to be the problem. What use is it to claim to have the facts if no-one is going to listen, I thought.

The sunflowers at least seemed to be nodding in agreement! They have a different agenda, I thought to myself. The sunflower is all about desire!

And aren't us humans really also about desires more than knowledge. We try to hide it, but it shows through. Babies and kids know better. For them, life is sniffing, sucking, licking, chewing, devouring, stroking, caressing, hugging, embracing!

Why don't we just look with wonder at the world? Why do we feel the need to suppress all those desires we had as kids when we become adults? So, sooner or later, we are caught up in a lie. Sooner or later we force ourselves to do things we hate and pretend to enjoy them, to tolerate people that we loathe rather than running away from them.

Before long we have forgotten what we really want and what we truly like. And when you do that you might as well say you've forgotten who you are.

I stretch one leg up towards the sky and put one arm back behind my head, arching my back and tilting my head. Yes, I'm thinking, it's an upside down world!

All of that desire sits in the body. We are always yearning, hungering, aspiring, lusting, relishing, savouring, admiring. We are in ecstasy or agony, melancholy or elation, boredom or fascination. Why deny it? Why not live our desires and be unashamed to tell other people how we really feel about our lives.

The sunflowers have got it right!

Emerald Web

Resting in a hammock, high up in a tree, some reflections on the nature of pleasure.

I had a tree house when I was a kid. Way high up in the branches, it seemed. I visit it now, as a grown-up, but cannot fit through its little doorway. Even so it brings back happy memories of days spent in leaves and sunlight. I've certainly not given up on this pursuit! Now though I've tied a big hammock in the branches, even higher off the ground, and I clamber up on sunny days to spend time with the trees and with my thoughts.

Today, strangely, I'm thinking about tattoos!

I'd clambered up to the hammock and now I lie here contemplating some henna tattoos just painted onto my skin. The shifting sunlight through the leaves mixes with the henna patterns. An emerald web of sunlight. It's hypnotic. Hennas are temporary of course, and one day I might get some permanent marks. But the whole notion of putting designs onto our skins had got me thinking.

Skin's a funny thing when you think about it. A surface onto the outside world. So the surface of it is not quite us, but not quite part of the outside world either.

When we draw or paint onto our skin we are kind of claiming it as our own. I am my body – we seem to be saying – I own my body. It's a defence against the world in a way, but also a statement. These images or words – the markings seem to be saying – are so important that I'm going to fuse them with my naked flesh. Some would say the tattooed body is never quite naked again – the images are always there as a kind of clothing. But I think I disagree. In a way we are more naked with our tatts. Not only are we baring flesh, we're baring our thoughts, our hopes, our art and our style as the images and words say who we are on the inside. That's vulnerability!

So why do it? You might be asking. Well, for me at least, it's about pleasure. Nude bodies can just be a bit boring. It's always more interesting to put on some markings or painting or writing!

And this gets me thinking about pleasure itself. What's that all about?

Three things come to mind straight away. There's knowledge, there's desire and then there's pleasure. Knowledge, I'm thinking, is what gets us into trouble! Humans are always living in their heads and inevitably each person thinks what's in their head is right. So maybe some other folk – even all other folk – are wrong. Trouble!

We are really all about desires – bodily desires. That's what all the knowledge and the thinking blots out. If we stopped to listen to our bodies we'd have a whole different view of the world and of ourselves.

At the same time though we can't just jump from one desire to another. We need to sort them, choose them, so we can have pleasure, happiness and joy.

The desires we indulge and the pleasures we choose – this is what defines who we are.

What though, you may be wondering, is the link back to tattoos? (Apart, of course, from tatts just being a pleasure in themselves?) Well, as I'd been thinking earlier, marking the skin is a two-way street. We claim ownership of our skin by marking it, but we also give those marks to the world as a gift. And touching is a two-way street as well, like none of the other senses. To touch is always to be touched in return.

I'm thinking something similar might happen with pleasure. Here's how that might go.

When we think of pleasure we mostly think in selfish ways. That we each try to maximise our own pleasure – that's an economist's view of the world!

Others will tell you there's no pleasure like shared pleasure. What would that be? Perhaps the liberal lefty's view of the world? Closer, but not there yet.

Instead I'm thinking of pleasure as a two-way street, like tatts and touch. It defines who we are – we own our own bodies through pleasure, but it can also be a gift. Giving pleasure might sometimes be like sharing pleasure, but it can also be very different.

Seems though – and perhaps you're with me on this one – that there's a bit of sacrifice involved in this. A gift I want to share with the world? Being pleasure for other people? Is that really what pleasure is about? (Or half of it anyway.)

And, 'giving pleasure'? Sounds a bit pervy as well!

The sun's gone behind a cloud. The canopy of leaves seems dark all of a sudden. But getting

in and out of this hammock is a big effort! I'll
just hang on in for a bit longer – see if I can
follow this train of thought to the end.

So let's try this:

Make someone laugh.

Make someone happy.

Make someone proud to be themselves.

Give someone care.

Give someone love.

And when I say 'someone' I guess I don't just
mean some other human. I think I need to
include the animals, the birds the fish the
insects the trees and the plants in all this too.
When we do these things we make ourselves
vulnerable. We are metaphorically naked for
other people and that invites others to be
comfortable with being themselves in return.

Still a big ask?

Well, I'm sticking with it!

Pleasure is a two-way street. Go write it on
your skin.

The Dreamtree

A magical tree offers possible glimpses of wisdom.

It's unusual to find this kind of tree growing out in the woods. They are normally in church yards these days. Once they might have been in sacred groves. Because these trees were seen as portals to a different world. Perhaps this particular tree is a remnant of an ancient grove, from the time when people really knew what trees are all about.

It's a warm still day. Perfect weather for visiting the tree. Sooz has taken an hour to walk here. It's a remote spot.

Every part of the tree is poisonous. Even so, it is used in small doses as a treatment for cancer. But that is not Sooz' purpose. The tree delivers another kind of medication on warm still days like today. The leaves of the tree give off a vapour when they are warmed by the sun. And if there is no breeze to carry it away then it lingers around the tree. It is there to be breathed in by anyone who stays close to the tree for long enough. It can even be infused through the pores of human skin.

So it's best to undress, and if you don't have a problem with getting naked then lying nude beneath the tree is certainly best. Sooz takes everything off and lies down. She's fully relaxed and looking up at the branches of the tree.

It's not long before the magic starts to happen. Normally Sooz would struggle to read a few sentences of a book before her concentration falters. She's brilliant at art and music but her brain just cannot get around words or arithmetic. Now though – and she knows this is the first step of the magic – her mind calms and changes to a more analytic perspective.

Everyone has their own myth and everyone has their own pursuit of pleasure. That's her first thought. It pops into her head with distinctive clarity – typical of the tree. Maybe it is enough to say that if life has given us pleasure then life has been worthwhile. But pleasure is an elusive thing – the thoughts continue. Pursuing it as if it were some kind of possession is likely to scare it away. We can try to hoard it for ourselves but then it is likely to dissolve in our hands.

Pleasure is a kind of two-way street. There are shared pleasures and there are pleasures that we can offer as a gift to others. But these views of pleasure also have their problems....

Sooz' eyes are closing now, but when she half-opens them again it seems there are colours swirling in the sky where once there had been leaves. The tree-inspired thoughts keep coming.

Shared pleasures have their own problems. It's something like assuming that someone who is on their own is lonely. Not many single tables in restaurants. You pay extra to go on holiday alone. At Christmas people tell the single person that no-one should be alone at

Christmas! In other words, they're a criminal! Shared pleasures is a phrase that conjures up all these images of enforced participation – team players, bonding, community! Phaaah!

But pleasure as a gift is problematic too. It seems like a life of altruism and sacrifice. Always trying to be generous and kind to everyone (even if that 'everyone' might reasonably include yourself). What if you did your best with all that your whole life and no-one even appreciated your efforts? There had to be something more!

Sooz sees the shapes of wildly-coloured growing and swirling things all around her now, which she sees whether her eyes are closed or open. The second phase was beginning.

What was that 'something more' that would make sense of things? The tree was ready to explain now – ready to reveal her hidden secrets.

There had to be something outside all these human rationalisations. Something that made it worthwhile for us to gift ourselves to each other. But that started to sound religious, and in entirely the wrong sort of way. Religion couldn't be about getting a 'reward' in heaven, or a reward on Earth for that matter. That is such an obviously bad motive that everyone just sees through it right away. Well, everyone of course apart form the folk who genuinely believe it! And of course they also believe that the reward is not for everyone...

Religions raise all the right questions. The answers though are poetic. That doesn't suit us too well these days. It doesn't even suit many religious people. But it's clever. Poetry is always there for personal interpretation and for different interpretations by cultures as times change.

So instead frame things in a more neutral way. The 'reward' has already been given, or to put it another way, the kingdom of heaven has already arrived. The universe has given us gifts first. Gifts for everyone, acknowledged or not.

A figure is appearing now in Sooz imagination. A figure who seems to hover just beyond an imaginary tree that has appeared now in place of the real one. It could be herself or her mother or her guardian angel – or all three of these. Were those wings towering over the figure? Or clouds? Or branches? The figure seems to urge Sooz on towards one final thought....

The gifts of the universe, the grace that is given – that is why we try to give pleasure to others. We need to pass those gifts along! That is the grace that is ours to give!

With this thought Sooz dream or vision takes over completely. She is lost in the images that the dreamtree conjures in her mind. She will wake, eventually, when the sun starts to set and all the dreams and visions will be almost fused into her skin.

But there was one final thought. One last thing the tree seemed to want to impart, in case she should wake up feeling smug that she had discovered some kind of 'Answer'. Remember where you started – the tree is saying. Everyone has their own myth. This too is a myth – this giving and receiving of grace. Live by it, or ignore it. It's your choice.

A Highland Re-enchantment

Two friends in the highlands of Scotland realise that the world needs to change.

I was visiting my friend Alistair on a winter's evening. It was then that the whole thing started. Alistair lived some five miles from my home where I lived with Janet. It was a walk by torchlight and in deep snow, although the night was clear. But I had not seen Alistair for many months, so I considered the lengthy walk worthwhile.

I remember he had cooked a haggis. We set to eating right away. There followed biscuits with a variety of cheeses. And of course, the whiskey. After the long walk and the heavy meal, the whiskey was welcome. Alistair and I had sat by his small fireplace, watching the logs crackle in the stove and catching up on each other's news.

It was then that he used the word.

'What we need Angus is a little more re-enchantment.'

Re-enchantment!

This is not a word that any highland man would think to be using. I had always thought of the mind of a highlander as being as clear and straight-forward as the fresh snow I had walked through on my way to Alistair's bothy. But here he was befuddling things with strange thoughts. Perhaps it was the whiskey, but I had to ask him.

'What is it that you mean by that Alistair?' I asked cautiously.

'Well', said Alistair, seeming to warm to his subject, 'time was that an Edinburgh squirrel could travel all the way to London without touching the ground.'

I was astonished. 'Now Alistair', I said, 'why on Earth would an Edinburgh squirrel want to go to London? Is it not bad enough for a squirrel to be living in Edinburgh?'

Alistair shook his head. 'No, no, Angus, you're missing the point. The point is that there were trees all the way. A continuous forest.'

This had caught my attention. 'Forest over most of England?' I asked.

'Yes, that's right', Alistair replied, 'And at that time most of Scotland too. That's what we've lost.'

'I never knew that Alistair. So what is this re-enchantment you speak of?'

'Well have you not noticed the changes over the last few years? The beaches we played on as wee boys are washed away. The glens are flooded. When it rains the rain comes in torrents. We have heatwaves that no-one has ever witnessed before. And then snow storms like today.'

'It's the government's fault', I said, but feeling unsure of myself. 'They should fix it.'

'Governments can't do much unless people really want change', Alistair replied. 'It's down to us. We need to re-enchant.'

There it was. That word again. What did Alistair mean?

'Think about it Angus. But now you must be off home to Janet.'

So I departed for the long trudge back home. But in truth I hardly noticed the walk as my mind was so taken up with what Alistair had said.

Forest. Over the whole of Scotland?

I reached home and went at once to bed. I lay beside Janet, both of us in our vests and with three downies – our normal winter bedding arrangements.

'Janet', I said in the darkness, 'Alistair said something strange tonight.'

'What did he say Angus?' She responded.

'He used a strange word. Re-enchantment.'

Janet made no response, so I continued. 'Do you know what it means Janet?'

'Angus', Janet replied at last. 'What is it I've been telling you for a good many years now?'

'Is it about putting out the bins correctly Janet?' I responded.

'No Angus. It's about the trees and the flowers, the birds, the animals, the insects.'

'What about them Janet?'

'They're all gone Angus!' said Janet, and the truth was beginning to sink in. 'We need to bring them back. And we need to love them, almost as if they were our own skin! That's re-enchantment Angus. That's what Alistair was meaning.'

I lay in silence in the darkness then as the full impact of what Alistair and then Janet had been telling me sank in.

Forest. Animals. Birds. Insects. Flowers.

How could we ever have thought to live without those things? How could we ever have let this happen?

I resolved that night to try to put things right, at least in our little corner of the world. I would visit Alistair again in the morning and together we would make a start.

Well that night is now some 40 years in the past, in 2032, and of course my readers will be aware of all the changes that have taken place in the world since then. Wars raged across the planet until finally it seemed there was nothing left to fight about and the Great Diaspora, as we now call it, settled down into their new homes in Antarctica and the lands close to the North Pole. We were forced into self-sufficiency, for the most part. Scotland more or less has no mainland to speak of. We are just a cluster of islands known now as the Caledonian Archipelago. And here in Caledonia we are lucky – or should I say, we were prudent. For Alistair and I had worked tirelessly throughout those terrible decades, finding the right species of tree, plant and animal to bring to our land and learning all we could of farming, food crops and animal husbandry to take us through what we knew was coming.

We have now what was once described as a Mediterranean climate, with all the trees and crops that go along with that. Olive groves, vineyards, orchards of peaches, apricots, plums, apples. A wild forest covers most of our islands with wild creatures in its midst.

Despite all our woes, the land is re-enchanted.

I am lying awake with Janet beside me in bed. We are oldsters now, but nonetheless we lie naked beneath a single sheet.

'What are you thinking Angus?' says Janet at my side.

There is the chirrup of insects from outside the

open window and I check that the mosquito net is tucked in around our mattress.

'I'm thinking that we did it', I say.

A swooshing sound from the long grass as a herd of deer passes near the house. Then the hoot of an owl.

'What Angus, what did we do?'

'This', I reply. 'This is what we did. Re-enchantment.'

Janet gives a low chuckle, almost as if she had known all along how things would turn out. Then she turns on her side and goes to sleep.

An audio version of *Alone in the Wood* is available on Youtube here:
https://youtu.be/HPQq_TGN3vI

An audio version of *A Highland Re-Enchantment* is available on Youtube here:
https://www.youtube.com/watch?v=okM_jMBgI
yU&t=13s

View an animation based on *The Dreamtree* here:
https://www.youtube.com/watch?v=GiBHtTDQR
gQ

Printed in Great Britain
by Amazon

26452077R00036